Tails from
the Bright Side

- a Dog's Life

Book 1

Let Sleeping Dogs Lie

by Kari Grace

DEDICATION

This is dedicated to the Lover of my soul, the One who saw worth and value in me when I saw nothing but shame, the One who chose to put breath in my body at birth when I was born dead.

ACKNOWLEDGEMENTS

Without my dearest darling man, Wolf, and my two sweet angels Alee and Sara, there would be little depth to anything I do. They have taught me about love in the hard places, regardless of cost. They have taught me what it means to live my faith.
I also thank God for our three fur babies – Rock, Little Bear, and Sasha – who, by entering my life, have also taught me much about love.

As with all her stories, this tale contains no foul language or sex scenes. Should you find biblical principles and scripture references more offensive than sex and profanity, this might not be the book for you.

CrossEffective Publishing©   copyright 2000
All rights reserved
ISBN: 978-0-9985355-1-7

Contents

About the Hero

My puppy loves much and licks much... so much so that a friend renamed him Sir Lick-a-Lot. Being the random redhead that I am, I started to think. I love what-ifs, so I developed a list.

What if dogs could talk? I mean for real talk, not just some psycho-analyst talk by a guy who studies dogs for a living and makes a hefty paycheck.

What if they had wishes, likes and dislikes? This mental meandering began when I first entered the world of dogs, by adopting what I affectionately call Rock. He and his friends did the most unreal things at a very real dog park, and I started to take note.

It might be an occupational hazard that comes with being a writer, but the dogs in my head became so real, I had to put down their adventures so they'd let me sleep at night.

In people world we refer to our animals as "pets". But what if dogs didn't know any better, and they did the same? What if, in dog world, people were the pets? What if dogs had personalities, favorite foods, favorite people, favorite music, favorite places? That might explain their seemingly erratic behavior at times.

These are the adventures of Rock the Mutt and his friends – some real, some imaginary – enjoying doggie life in Hope Springs, and his effect those close at hand, human and canine alike. Or, in his own words, "Puppy Power!"

Creating a disturbance wherever he goes he's lovable, gentle, and oh, so adorable. Big ears, big feet, kind eyes, great sense of humor; easy to love, hard to hate, what's not to like?

It is also my humble attempt to share the goings-on in my head over the space of three years, while friends and loved ones shook their head and thought me rather strange. Perhaps I am. Welcome to my world. Hope you enjoy the trip. K

Before the Beginning

The heavy wooden door opened and all sunlight disappeared as the large frame of a rather handsome young man in army fatigues entered the room.

Posters covered the yellow walls.

The sound of woofs and meows made him pause a moment, as he wiped a tear away.

The small receptionist smiled her brightest smile and said in her perkiest voice,

"Welcome to One Last Chance. How may I help you?"

His attention was diverted by some shuffling going on at his feet, followed by a sharp yelp. He looked up and smiled a sad smile.

"I'm about to deploy on a 12 month tour overseas that could well turn into 16. I need to make sure my puppy is taken care of. Hopefully even adopted."

The petite blond behind the counter moved some papers from one side of the desk to the other.

"Absolutely. We're very good at that," she purred, gazing into his eyes as she smiled her brightest smile.

"He's a good dog. Lovable. Affectionate. Loyal. Kind of." Another yelp came from the floor.

"Wonderful." She stood, and reached to put a clipboard on the solid oak counter.

"But I feel it only fair to warn you, he has strange tastes in food."

"Oh, really?" Her eyebrows lifted slightly.

"Yes ma'am. He loves fresh carrots. Big ones. Long ones."

"I see. That's... not too strange."

He looked at her sheepishly.

"I should say he loves food, period. But especially carrots. And other things. Soap."

The distraction at his feet barked once. Loudly.

"Excuse me, did you say ..."

🐾

"Yes, ma'am, I'm afraid I did."

"Well," said the receptionist, looking slightly confused but still trying to look cute, "that's a little unusual, but I'm sure he's wonderful."

The handsome soldier scooped up the small black and tan ball of fur just to prove the point.

"Ah... yes...", stammered the rather flustered receptionist as she tried hard to smile her brightest smile.

"Please complete this release form and we'll see what we can do."

She turned her back on him and went back to her papers.

"You *are* a no-kill center, right?" the soldier added. Concern flickered in his large brown eyes.

"Sir, we're an animal shelter, some call us The Pound; we're the only one around, but no, I'm afraid we do not 100% guarantee that."

His face fell as he rubbed his left temple.

"I'm out of options. Due to ship out any day. I don't know what to do."

She pushed the clipboard closer to his hand.

His eyes filled with tears.

Bowing his head, the soldier mumbled softly, "Lord, please make sure Rock gets adopted. It'll break my heart if he isn't. I can't take care of him where I'm going, and I love the goofball. He's weird, but he's a good dog. Send him to the right family."

He turned silently, sat on a nearby bench, and started completing the paperwork as tears rolled down his cheeks unchecked. He didn't even notice.

The Start of it All

It had been a long time since Rock had felt the touch of a human hand. Or even a foot, come to think about it. The Pets in the pound tended to ignore him as much as possible, but since Rock was high energy that was next to impossible. His biggest weakness? Over-excitement when one came near enough to lick.

The pound Pets didn't quite know what to make of him. Especially the big ones, with the deep voices and hairy paws.

Yep, Rock was most definitely a people-person-dog. He was also a sucker for a warm ankle. Preferably one rubbed down with lotion.

All his dreams came true the day he met his very own personal Pet. As far as Rock was concerned, it was love at first bite.

Joy had been hankering for a kitten for ever. She'd finally talked her big sister into a trip to the local pound. Faith blamed those big brown eyes of hers. Strange how all the sisters were so very different, yet all sprang from the same gene pool. Joy, sandy blond hair, brown eyes so dark they evoked the sense of falling gently into a bottomless pit. Grace, jet black hair, eyes the grey of skies hiding a tempest brewing. Mercy, auburn hair, startling blue eyes, the envy of every girl at the senior prom. Hope, chestnut hair, emerald green eyes bright as jewels. Last and most definitely least, average Faith with her average hazel eyes and average muddy brown hair. Which, at this precise moment, she brushed furiously, taking out all her pent-up frustration at being talked into one more bright idea by her older sibling on her poor head. She wondered afresh how this latest sister caper would end, as a vague feeling crept over her of being dragged

🐾

into yet one more thing she wasn't quite prepared for.
She was right.

The day began as usual with the pound Pets going
from cage to cage distributing breakfast. Which,
naturally, Rock wolfed down like there was no
tomorrow.
He was always hungry, yet rarely full. There were
never any left-overs in Rock's bowl for the other mutts
to eat which some of the bigger dogs took exception to
but had learned to accept.
This bright Spring morning Rock sniffed the air
expectantly. His head raised higher, his ears perked
up, and he sniffed once again just to make sure.
Two Pets were walking past the animal cages. One
definitely seemed to prefer cats but Rock knew how to
use those big soulful eyes; he'd had four long months
to practice.
"Which kitten do you like, Joy?" asked Faith.
"I'll know her when I see her," came the vague reply.
"Oh, it's a 'her', is it?"
"Most definitely," Joy answered with a grin that
charmed even the hardest heart.
Faith was finding it hard to ignore the large furball
going nuts in the corner cage. He almost seemed
fixated on her, as if he realized she was considering
adopting too. Not a huge black and tan ball of energy,
of course; something more sedate, a dog she could go
walking with, maybe snuggle up to on cold winter
nights.
Then again, he did have a way about him.
Before long Faith had cracked..
The biggest pound Pet walked toward the cage with a
leash. The one Rock had named Chubby. Rock did

his best to sit.

"This is a good thing," thought Rock, trying desperately to contain his excitement. It was either time for a walk or, as he suspected, the Pet he'd had his eye on had picked him.

"Come on, nuisance, you're finally out of here!" Chubby extended his hand, carefully attaching the leash to Rock's collar.

Rock smiled, stood, and promptly bit the hand in front of him.

Then, before Chubby could slam the cage door shut, Rock was off, a black streak aiming for the pretty Pet with such trouble looking him in the eye. Crash! He collided with her unsuspecting knees, sending Faith to the gravel path. She sat there for a minute, as Chubby sheepishly handed her Rock's leash, asking her once again if she was, "sure about this?"

All three walked to the office and Faith completed the adoption papers. Chubby wished her good luck in a rather ominous tone that had her slightly worried.

Close Encounters of the Canine Kind

It was a bright sunny day in Hope Springs. Life in the mid-west tended to be that way. Rock had spent the most wonderful morning chewing on his Pet's shoes, diving in the trash, eating half a bar of oatmeal soap, and munching on the grapefruit she didn't mean to leave out on the counter.

He was now "in the doghouse" for the third time that morning, according to Faith, a fact that didn't bother him in the least. He was all dog.

Rock had only lived with his new Pet for one week but had made himself at home immediately. As she grabbed his leash yet again, Rock sniffed the air and sighed a contented doggy sigh. Life was good. He was getting used to Faith, though Faith doubted she'd every quite get used to Rock. However, she was not a quitter. Lesser mortals may be, but not Faith.

He licked his leash and sat at the door. He waited while she opened the car door, and his ears perked up. An open door usually meant a trip somewhere.

"In!" commanded Faith confidently. Rock smiled, and obeyed.

Once on the highway he stuck his big head out of the window, as usual. Faith had come to the conclusion he liked the feel of wind in his ears.

"I hope we're finally going to visit that muddy place," he thought to himself.

Had he but known it, that muddy place was known by the locals as the Hope Springs Municipal Dog Park, and was indeed their destination.

In a few short minutes they had arrived.

Rock humored his Pet as Faith again commanded him to "stay" before putting her hand on the ancient metal gate leading to the muddy expanse beyond.

This was their third outing together and he wasn't

making it easy on her.

"Good boy!" Faith cooed as he did his best to sit still till she released him.

Oh yeah. Like taking candy from a baby. He had her fooled.

All the dogs this side of the fence were eager to meet the newbie.

At least, Rock hoped it was 'meet' on their minds, and not 'eat'.

Two Huskies looked particularly scary.

As Faith pushed open the gate Rock realized it would be useless to resist.

Let the sniff-fest begin.

Rock took off toward the biggest mud puddle and before long had made a friend.

Oakley was everything Rock wasn't. Tall, skinny yet solid, even funny in a goofy kind of way, and very, very obedient. Rock didn't have that problem. Still, for all their differences, they got on like a doghouse on fire.

As they leaped and bounded and chased each other's tails Faith sat on a bench next to Rick Danger, and watched and waited to see what would happen next. With Rock, there was always something happening next.

A small white dog appeared from right field.

"Halloo, laddie," he snuffled in a distinctly Scottish brogue.

"McTavish is the name. Ye'r new here, are ye not?"

"Yes, I'm..."

One of the large grey huskies nudged the small dog aside, got in Rock's face and glared at him.

"Oooo... are yooo?" he growled in a Russian accent.

"Rock," panted Rock.

"Vell, you better calm down or you end up at za bottom of za 'Ope Springs river."

He snarled menacingly, showed his teeth, then promptly turned his butt on the newest member of the Hope Springs Municipal Dog Park.

"What's a river?" asked Rock.

"Ignore him," woofed his brand new new best puppy pal in the world.

"That's just Mishka. Mishka and Moutar are Reikah's heavies, but we mostly ignore them. Don't' let them know you're rattled."

"I'm not rattled," barked Rock defensively. "What's rattled?"

A large Alsatian wandered up, sniffed Rock's butt, receiving a snap near his ear for his trouble.

"My bad. Name's Feingold, and I'm a PD. Preacher's Dog, for the uninitiated."

He looked expectantly at Rock.

"Break it down, bro! I told you, you's in the hood here! We ain't all from the soft side of the tracks," growled Oakley, taking off for the nearest mud puddle.

Feingold continued to stare at Rock, who shrugged his haunches nonchalantly, bounding after Oakley.

Until something stopped him dead in his tracks. The most beautiful thing on four legs had just sauntered out from behind a large oak tree.

"Well hello, handsome," she woofed in a soft voice, batting her eyes at him brazenly.

"Wh... wh... who are you?" asked Rock, jaws hanging open, tongue lolling sideways.

"Godiva," grinned the Afghan hound, again batting big brown eyes.

"And I'm Beaker," came another voice as a small

🐾

brown and white beagle leaped in from the left.

Oh wow. Rock was in shock. He never imagined such beautiful creatures existed. The dog pound had been full of dogs, every size and breed, but these two girls were in a league of their own.

As he looked from one to the other, all he could think was, "you lucky dog, you!"

Looking into Beaker's dark eyes his heart fluttered in his chest.

"Must have been that left-over meatloaf I ate this morning," Rock mumbled under his breath. All of a sudden he was tongue-tied. And Rock was never tongue-tied.

"This is Rock." Godiva smiled and walked regally toward the nearest water bucket, head held high, delicately avoiding a big mud puddle. There were several around, since it had rained for the last three days straight. Which explained all the canine energy. Beaker glanced at Rock one last time and took off running, Rock panting but close behind, McTavish bringing up the rear. Maverick the Wire Fox Terrier and Colt the Boxer were in the mix around the middle somewhere, Colt reaching for Rock's tail.

Faith wasn't sure if she should intervene.

Rick Danger simply smiled.

A Check Up from the Butt Up

The warm breeze wafted through the screen door as Rock lay lazily in the sunshine.

"Today we're taking a trip to the V-E-T," Faith announced proudly.

"You need a check-up from the butt up, and probably an overhaul too, after all that soap!"

Rock obediently jumped into the red Beetle Bug, though he didn't care much for the tone in her voice.

Ten minutes later they arrived at a small brick building. Rock could hear barking. This was the strangest dog park he had ever seen. Not that he was an expert on the subject; he'd only seen two in his whole short life.

They walked through the large double doors and, to Rock's delight, he saw people!

Some were sitting, some were standing, but all were unprepared. He strained at the leash in a frenzied attempt to lick the nearest ankle. Faith had learned a thing or two in the three weeks since her new house guest had moved in, so she kept a tight grip on the leash.

"Oh no you don't, Mister!" she said, using her best Alpha Dog voice.

"So not happening."

Collapsing onto a bench she continued to hold his leash tight, no matter how hard he pulled and whined. She was a small woman and had to use most of her strength to keep him from licking the exposed kneecap to her right.

After half an hour of whimpering, a Pet in a white coat called Rock's name and once again Faith had to keep him from licking the nearest hand.

"Follow me, please," said the young veterinary assistant as she led them down a back hall.

"Have a seat," she said to Faith, then smiled at Rock. "Would you like a treat, young man?"

Rock didn't know much, and he was discovering new things every day, but one thing he *did* know was the word, "treat". He wolfed it down like he hadn't been fed in weeks.

"Hungry, are you?" the lady asked as she desperately tried to weigh the wriggling mass of black and brown fur. Rock wasn't sure he liked being weighed.

"He always is," mumbled Faith.

"My name's Sue," the assistant said to no one in particular, proudly pointing to her name tag.

"There's a good boy," Sue cooed, ruffling his ears and giving Rock another treat, which promptly went the same way as the first.

She did a few more tests, rewarding him the same way.

After the fifth treat Sue cried in expiration, "did ya even taste it?!"

Faith smiled; she knew the feeling well. Rock was a bottomless pit.

"You should see him eat breakfast," she whispered.

Rock decided he did *not* like the man in the white coat who smelled funny, and he most *definitely* did not like that silver thing the man called a 'rectal thermometer'. Just to prove his point, he bit the hand that held it. Then, because he was Rock, he farted. Twice.

"I apologize on his behalf," Faith said sheepishly.

"Do you mean his be*hind*?" the kindly veterinarian chuckled, offering a smile.

Faith couldn't help but laugh, though she still felt mortified.

"Are you new here?" she asked, trying hard to change

the subject.

"As a matter of fact I am," beamed the good doctor and stuck out his hand.

"We've not been formally introduced. I'm Jonathan. But Jon'll do just fine."

"Thank you for your patience," she mumbled as Rock adjusted his legs and farted yet again.

"Don't worry, it's very normal dog behavior," Doctor Jon said gently, playing with Rock's jowls.

Faith doubted that strongly.

The doctor smiled again, and this time the smile reached all the way up towards his ears.

Another Fine Mess

After being cooped up in the vet's office for several hours Faith felt it wise as a responsible dog owner to swing by the Hope Springs Municipal Dog Park on the way home, so Rock could get his wiggles out. Rock always seemed to have a lot of wiggles.

They arrived at the gate just as five dogs decided to act as a self-appointed welcoming committee, and came to sniff the newly-vaccinated Rock, who gave up all resistance after one look at Moutar.

He'd come to accept the sniff-fest as a fact of life at the Hope Springs Municipal Dog Park.

Within two minutes they had all lost interest, trotting off toward a fight developing in the far south corner.

A minute later Rock's best friend Oakley bounded up to him with a stick in his mouth, spit flying with each bound. Rock let out an excited yelp.

"Dude! You're here! I've been cooped up in the apartment forever and I missed you!"

"It's been two days, gringos. And it was raining. Pets never go out in ze rain – don'chu know anysing?" woofed Padré, the Chihuahua.

Oakley stuck his nose in the air, turned and took off, with his best doggie friend right behind. Both made straight for the biggest mud puddle around, much to the chagrin of their respective Pets. McTavish, being the Scottish Highland Terrier that he was, quickly followed suit.

Godiva merely huffed, then proceeded to delicately lick her left front foreleg while Beaker made a dash for the developing huddle in the middle of the puddle, and before the friends realized it, half the dogs in the park had decided to party hearty with them.

The mud puddle was fast becoming too overcrowded for Rock's tastes, so he got up to leave, bringing quite a bit of the mud puddle with him as he limped away, head down.

"You've got to be kidding me!" shrieked Faith as the dog she didn't always claim slunk toward her.

"Cut loose and cut a rug!" squeaked Chang Po, a Pekinese, up to his knees in slush.

"I don't believe I will, thank you," came a low guttural growl from the left.

"Are you serious?!" asked Rock.

"Well, actually, I am," barked the rather large ball of fuzz standing next to Padré. The Sheepdog smiled.

Oakley leaned over and woofed softly in Rock's ear, "Dude, his *name* is Serious."

All Rock could do was stare.

His Pet, however, had other ideas.

Rock smelled bad, and Faith had finally had enough so she decided to take matters into her own hands.

"Bath is good. Bath is fun. Bath is healthy. Bath is necessary. So you're gonna have one!"

Rock was not convinced that 'bath' was good, fun, healthy *or* necessary. And he was most certainly not convinced he was going to have one.

To prove his point he made a beeline for the mud pit slap bang in the middle of the Hope Springs Municipal Dog Park.

"Rock!" yelled Faith but, as usual, her words fell on deaf ears.

"That's it! We're *so* through!"

She glared at Rock's retreating backside.

"Oh-oh dude. You done done it now!" woofed Beaker.

"I told you young whippersnappers; nothing good comes from running. Obedience is best – I should know... I was young once..."

The General looked down his snout at Rock who had, by now, made it to the edge of the mud pit.

"Don't do it dude," warned Oakley.

It was too little too late. Momentum had built up and Rock couldn't stop if he tried. Which he didn't. So of course he landed with a splat in the deepest part of the mud.

For the third time that day Faith found herself at a loss for words.

Rick Danger simply smiled.

After much pulling and several carrots, Faith got Rock into the car and drove home silently fuming. Rock was starting to get scared. Very scared.

Throwing the front door open, Faith dragged Rock down the hallway into a room he'd never been in before. Then she closed the door. Now he just wasn't scared. He was terrified.

Next, she started taking off her fur. Rock didn't know Pets could do that. He couldn't. She turned on the water and shoved Rock into the bath; he immediately, frantically, jumped right out again.

"I *told* you," Faith said defiantly, "you're getting a bath!"

She yanked him back into the tub and tied the leash so tight around the faucet it almost strangled him. Rock realized the more he struggled, the tighter the chain became. He finally calmed down and gave in as Faith poured stinky stuff all over him. Miserable, he howled to make his feelings known but she had learned the hard way that she could make him stay when she really needed him to.

As she scrubbed every inch of his fur she softly hummed to herself, very pleased with the way this bath was progressing. She rinsed him off with warm water, loosened the leash and climbed out, with Rock not far behind. He promptly shook himself as hard as he could.

"Rock!" screamed Faith. "Hold on a minute!"
Grabbing a towel she rubbed him hard all over, then opened the door. Rock made a run for the border. Or the front door. Whichever came first.

Like Father, Like Nun

Feingold was not having a very successful day.
He was old, and rather deaf, but living with Father
Fred and Sister Ann for the last 10 years had taught
him a thing or two. The combination of reclusive
priest and outgoing nun had finally taken a toll on the
Alsatian, namely, that all the dogs in the dog park
thought him a little shy of a dog biscuit or two, if you
know what I mean, but they loved him anyway.

He knew it was important, and he'd tried several
times to tell his friends what Father Fred told Pets
over and over again. They were all in big trouble and
they had to give their heart to the Dog who loved
them, the Dog who gave all He had to be their best
friend, but it kept coming out wrong. Father Fred said
it so much better.

Feingold took a deep breath and tried again.

"In the beginning, Dog created the heavens and the
earth..."

"What's a heavens?" asked Rock as he and Oakley
sped by in a valiant attempt to catch Snitch, a small
white dog of questionable heritage.

"I'm never quite sure, but he means well," Oakley
huffed, front paws stretched out, almost reaching
Snitch's twitching tail.

Leo the Golden Retriever decided to join in the fun.
Which was unusual; normally he just lay under the
trees or sat near the nutty nun, watching the goings-
on in the Hope Springs Municipal Dog Park.

A Huskey came up from behind, calmly sniffing
Rock's butt without reservation.

"Listen 'ere, runt. Da Boss don't like ya, we don't like
ya, so ya watch yaw snout or ya'll be sleepin' wid da
fishes!"

"What's fishes?" asked Rock of the retreating

🐾

backside.

"Don't mind Mishka and Moutar. They're just bullies," Beaker woofed kindly.

With that, she took off toward the largest oak tree, confident the boys would follow right behind. Which, of course, they did.

Feingold was tuckered out. He'd been trying to explain how serious the trouble was, but his friends didn't seem to understand. He finally gave up for the day.

After that he and Beaker chased Padré for quite a while, and now the old dog needed a break. His bones couldn't do what they used to.

So he took one. A break. Right then and there. Dead in the middle of the dog park.

When Padré realized their friend had bugged out he pulled up and looked around, sniffing.

"There he is!" barked Beaker, as she and the Chihuahua made a beeline for the large grey Alsatian.

"W'assup, dog?" asked Beaker when she'd caught her breath.

"I'm just all pooped out," Feingold whined tiredly.

"Very funny," joked Padré.

"For real. I need a rest. And I have a question."

Beaker and Padré looked at t their friend Alsatian expectantly.

"What?" asked Padré.

"I don't get it. What's the deal with Leo and Snitch? The little guy's ok... kind of, but the big guy..."

"His woofer's wore out." Beaker looked sad.

"Do what?" asked Feingold, confused.

"Yeah, dog, 'e lead a rough life. Seen sings... done sings... jou don' wanna know."

Padré looked around to make sure nodog was with within earshot.

"Yeah. But Snitch? *His* yapper works just fine. Unfortunately." Beaker growled softly.

"Zat's why they call 'im Snitch! 'Cos he tattles all ze time!" Padré smiled at his bad joke.

Actually, it was true. Snitch really had got the name from his owner, an informant who worked with Leo and his Pet Josh.

The fact of the matter was, the other canines didn't see why but the two dogs made a good team, just like their Pets, even if they were on opposite sides of the law.

Beaker was happy to tell what she knew, and when she was done her friend settled down on his haunches, looking thoughtful.

"Wow." Feingold didn't know quite what to say. He'd been with the Father and the nutty Nun so long he couldn't remember a time when he'd lacked food... or a doghouse. They told him he'd been found in a graveyard and been brought to Father Fred as a two-week old pup, but he was too young to remember. All he knew was that he loved the reverend and the nutty nun, and he never wanted to live anywhere else on earth. Ever.

Leo's Tale

Leo was somedog it was hard to get to know. In fact, he had very few friends. The only dog who seemed to get through to him at all was a pup who went by the name of Snitch.

Leo wasn't his real name of course, but with a Pet on the Hope Springs Police Force, what did you expect? For, as every dog knows, the local 'leo' was everyone's friend. Hence the name.

Leo's Pet Josh had a partner, Jenks, who didn't seem to like dogs in general but humoured Leo.

Both dogs went out with their Pets to do exciting things in law enforcement, very secret hush-hush missions; they told everydog who was curious they could *tell* them but then they'd have to *kill* them. At which point the canines in the dog park stopped asking.

Snow had fallen the previous night and most sensible Pets and their dogs were inside, where every dog worth his bark should be. Not Leo and Snitch.

Leo lived in a large house on the edge of town with his very own fenced-in back yard; the other canines were at a loss to explain his passion for the Hope Springs Municipal Dog Park when he had the room to run. Then again, it probably had to do with Snitch. Which wasn't *his* real name either, but nodog could pronounce the real one.

Leo and Snitch were indeed a strange pair but they worked well together, both on the job and off. Friendly canine competition had developed over the years as to which partner dog had saved the other's life the most, today being a prime example.

You'd think a quiet town like Hope Springs wouldn't have much crime. But you'd be wrong. It turned out the town was the half-way stop-off point for gangs and thugs on the drug road from New York to Florida. Who knew? The Hope Springs Police Force, apparently, which explained why Leo and Snitch were out playing in the snow before sunrise. Kind of.

Today had begun long before dawn, as it often did, waking with a phone call as an alarm clock. Jenks had phoned to ask Josh and Leo to meet him downtown outside the Café au Lait. José had news, and the two boys in blue desperately needed a break in the case; it was fast becoming headline news.

Josh preferred Java the Hut, but he knew Jenks was a creature of habit. And Josh never said no to a free coffee and donut. For that matter, neither did Leo. Which explains how two perfectly sane men in uniform with two slightly muddy dogs came to be sitting in the dark in snowdrifts on main street sipping hot coffee, profusely thanking BonBon LeFleur, owner of the café, for opening up early.

"You owe me za favor big time," she complained, then added under her breath, "Sacré bleu!" as she locked the store front door, turning to walk home.

Leo licked his front paw and looked at BonBon lazily.

"I'll remember this the next time Henri gets a traffic ticket, I promise," Jenks offered, giving her one of his biggest smiles, the ones he usually reserved for the ladies.

She snorted, walked five more steps, and stopped two doors down. As she pulled out the apartment key she added,

"You boys need anysing else, you 'ave to wait till 8. You better be glad je vous aime."

"We love you too, BonBon," both boys in blue responded in unison. They loved their town, and would gladly give their very lives to make it a safe place for folks like BonBon and Henri, not to mention BonBon's three Great Danes and a Persian.

As he took another swig of his coffee, Jenks whispered, "It's a tough job…"

"… but somebody's got to do it," finished Josh. Leo's ears suddenly stood erect as both men exchanged a cautious glance around Main Street.

Out of the shadows stepped a terrified and disheveled José, followed by an extremely nervous Snitch.

"We gotta talk, man."

Snitch's Story

Snitch grew up on the hard side of the tracks, and that's where he stayed. He knew the streets, ran the streets, and played the streets. His first week of life was a fight for everything he got – food, attention, petting – so he made it his mission to distinguish himself above all the other 'hood dogs, a goal he achieved early on.

Snitch was originally from Ecuador but had been dognapped from his native land and dogsmuggled into America by way of Moldova. No one could pronounce his real name. Snitch would've been a victim of dogtrafficking if he hadn't slipped his collar and got away. José had found him asleep beside a lamppost in New York when he went to buy lunch during a sting operation gone bad in his early days as an informant. They'd been inseparable ever since.

Snitch was known in the 'hood as, "the dog you don't mess with", and for good reason. He'd seen things, done things, things he wasn't proud of. But realized it came with the territory. He was, after all, the only informant's pup on the block, which was enough in and of itself to give a dog paws for thought. He wasn't quite sure what an 'informant' did, exactly, but his pet was proud to be one and since José was good to him, Snitch rarely asked questions.

People Pets came and went at odd hours, making the small apartment often look and smell like the local lowlife hangout. Anyone with secrets to discuss, it seemed to Snitch that 621C Butchers Lane was the place to be for anything shady. He wasn't quite sure if he liked that state of affairs or not but hey, it was what it was. Not that the visitors ever brought their pups, it was always just the Pets. Luckily Snitch actually liked people Pets. In fact, when he was in a playful mood he was the most delightful and friendly canine you could ever hope to meet. On a good day. On a bad day, it was a whole' nother story. When the PTD (or Puppy Terror Disease, according to José) kicked in, there was simply no telling what Snitch would do. José said it was nobody's fault, and that, 'that's what bein' raised on the streets will do to ya.'

To look at his coat you would think Snitch a purebred Yorkshire Terrier, but looks can be deceiving. His mother had denned with multiple partners, always seemed to fall for the bad boy dogs; he'd heard tell she met her death at the jaws of her latest lover, but who was Snitch to judge? She'd delivered many a litter in her time, but none of the pups looked alike. She moved around a lot, and he never met his sire, Roberto, who, apparently, had a rep of his own to protect - he didn't hang around long after Snitch's birth, since pups cramped his style.

Glad to be free of his dognappers and refusing to be used for a bait dog, Snitch didn't really like being homeless but grudgingly accepted this state of affairs until the day José found him and brought him to the small town of Hope Springs. Then Snitch's world began to change for the better.

For one thing, now he had to stay on the right side of the law. His Pet may not always be on the up and up, but José kept his nose clean and expected Snitch to do the same. For another, friendship between José and Josh and Jenks ran deep, forged over the space of five tough years. In their own way, each of the three men would willingly give their life for the other, regardless of what side of the law it would put them on. Snitch had to respect a friendship like that.

This explains how three almost sane men and two slightly strange dogs came to be having an informal breakfast meeting in a snowdrift on Main Street, two cups of coffee and five donuts between the five hungry males.

DownDammit!

Beaker was very excited. After just completing her first class in doggie CPR training she wanted to practice on Gunny, the Schnauzer, but he would have none of it.

"Heck, no! There are things a pal does, and things a pal doesn't, and that's one of them," he growled as he walked away to find a pinecone to chew on.

As she looked around Beaker she saw that Finklestein the Border Collie was not quite himself today. He was brooding, lying listless in the dirt. Normally he was the first one to play fetch.

"What's wrong, Finklestein?" she asked in her most concerned voice.

Several other dogs wandered over as soon as they realized there was something not quite right in the Hope Springs Municipal Dog Park. He sniffed loudly. "I used to think my name was Finklestein, but now I'm starting to wonder if it might be DownDammit! That's what my Pet's been calling me lately." He had tears in his eyes.

"Well, you do get a little excited but I'm sure she doesn't mean it. Pets know how important a dog's name is to him – it shows his nature. She wouldn't just change it without telling you. Don't be mad at her. She's the hand that feeds you."

Beaker laid a small paw softly on his large one in sympathy, while some of the other dogs nodded in agreement.

"What do you know?!" Finklestein snapped angrily.

"A whole lot. Several broken relationships, and a 'Rock'y one now, but I'm tryin'."

The other dogs snickered. It was common knowledge the pup was in love with the newest member of Hope Springs Municipal Park – she had it bad! But he was

🐾

clueless. Such a dingbat.

"He's a puppy, dog! He don't get it. He will," barked Feingold.

"Seriously, you pups really need to grow up," woofed Godiva with her nose in the air.

"Dang, gurl, for a hot dog you shaw is ugly!" Oakley smiled.

"Hot dog... get it?"

Godiva simply groaned, turned, and stalked away.

"Well, you know what they always say," barked Serious.

"No," groaned all the dogs, "what do they always say?"

"A bird in the hand is worth two in the bush."

As usual no dog in the dog park understood him.

Chang Po dashed off, grabbed a ball, dropped it at Finklestein's front paw, and wagged his tail. He knew just what his bdp (best doggie pal) needed.

A game of chase-the-ball solved everything in life, as far as Chang Po was concerned.

Finklestein put on a happy face for the sake of his small friend, grabbing the ball in his mouth.

Rock didn't miss the pound one bit; he was having another wonderful day free and carefree.

Faith, however, was not. From sheer self-defense and to preserve her sanity she decided to take him to his second favorite place on earth, the Hope Springs Municipal Dog Park.

(His first favorite place was, of course, her kitchen, complete with a very full dog bowl and quite a bit of stolen leftovers, ideally straight from the fridge. He dreamed of it on a regular basis.)

After watching Godiva be her usual ladylike self, and Feingold also be himself – strange but likable – Rock

went in search of Sugar, the tomboy Pit Bull who let
him wrestle with her to his heart's content. He
discovered she'd left fifteen minutes ago.
"Bummer, man," snickered Leo the golden retriever.
Snitch just watched and waited.
"She's cute and fun, not weird or boring or prissy,"
responded Rock, casting a glance in Godiva's
direction.
Rock was about to wonder what to do next when he
spotted a large expanse of solid muscle barreling
toward him. Maverick had hardly got through the
gate when he spied Rock, took off, and tackled his
friend to the ground, latching on to Rock's right ear.
Faith watched cautiously and when she saw no blood,
looked over at Maverick's owner.
Rick Danger simply shrugged his shoulders as if to
say, "Boys will be boys," then gave that rather
disarming smile of his.
"Will 'sorry' help?"
"Not really."
"How about dinner?"
Faith swallowed her frustration and forced a smile. It
was hard to be mad at somebody who'd treated her
like a baby sister most of her life.
"Sure," she said grudgingly.

Bad News Travels

José couldn't stop twitching. He was shaking like a leaf. Josh and Jenks had been told something bad was going down but the Hope Springs Police Force had no clue what. Or when. José talked rapidly, becoming more and more animated; Jenks sensed a gang war had begun, and it was taking place on *their* turf.

Both boys in blue listened intently to what their informant and long-time friend had to say.

Rumour had it that, the oldest son of the Pitt boss had fallen hard for a daughter of the Bulls, something the rival gangs didn't take too well. "Stick to your own," had always been an unwritten rule on the streets, and these two kids had broken it. For love, no less. Risking their very lives for passion. Josh sighed and shook his head. There had been unrest for decades between the Pitts and the Bulls –the violence was intensifying, if the rumours were true, with a showdown bound to happen sooner or later.

It looked like this history-making event just might happen in Hope Springs.

The two officers looked at one another with fear in their eyes.

"How come you know so much, José?" Josh asked gently. He'd never seen his friend like this, and was more concern than he cared to admit.

Leo came over and licked José's face, as if he could understand what was going on. Snitch just sat.

"I know more than you think about the Pitts and the Bulls.

🐾

Carlos is my father."

José hung his head sadly.

"Carlos?! As in the Pitt boss? You gotta be kidding me!" Jenks couldn't help himself. When experiencing shock he became more vocal than normal.

Snitch gave a loud bark, as if he understood.

Josh knew José had a history – everyone has a past, even an informant – but this... he would never have guessed.

"The rumble's goin down, man. Real soon. Not sure when, but I know where. The park."

"As in *our* park? Out in the open like that?" Josh broke in.

"That's the word on the street, yeah. They like to do business in the open, keep it all above-board."

"Right, criminals always do their nefarious acts in the open; makes no sense to do it under cover of darkness where they can't be seen!" Jenks was still trying to accept what José was sharing.

"I don't know about all that, man. All's I know is it's goin' down. Real soon. You two better be ready for anythin'. It's gonna get bloody."

"Oh boy. We're in deep doo doo," mumbled Jenks.

"Yep," confirmed Josh.

Snitch couldn't wait to get to the dog park. He grabbed the

first ear he saw.

"Hey, dog, you gotta listen. There's a rumble goin' down in Hope Springs and we better be watchin' out for strangers in town." He let go her ear abruptly.

Sugar glared at the little white Terrier like he had lost his ever-loving mind. Then her eyes lit up.

"We're safe here. The dog park is the safest place a canine can be. Maybe we should stay the night, have a sleepover."

Snitch could see he wasn't getting the reaction he wanted, so he moved on.

Mishka and Moutar were rolling in a mud puddle close by, so Snitch took off, eager to share his news.

Neither of the Huskies were impressed.

"Vot 'as dat got to do wid *us?*" Moutar growled menacingly.

Snitch tried one more time. He bounded up to McTavish, the one dog known to all as the most resourceful amoung them.

After Snitch had told his tale yet again, McTavish scratched his ear thoughtfully.

"We need a plan, laddie. A plan that'll keep every canine safe and sound and all in one piece!"

"I'm calling a meeting of the Four."

Snitch looked at his friend in horror. "The Four?"

"It's gone way beyond us, laddie. Time to call in the big

🐾

guys. They'll know what to do."

"No way, dog. We gotta get some place safe and hide. It's every dog for himself!" Snitch barked as he ran toward the bench where he'd left his Pet. José was gone.

It's All in the Tail

Fall had arrived early in Hope Springs. Leaves were turning and the town was at its most beautiful. The Fall Frolic was in full swing as far as the town was concerned, and almost everyone who was anyone, Pets and canines alike, were to be found sitting outside Java the Hut, licking on fresh made ice-cream waffle cones.

With the day of the Greatest Tail Ever Dog Show- the annual event no self-respecting canine would miss, just one week away, Pugsley was in fine form. He was determined, as usual, to win it. And, as usual, so was Godiva. It had become a source of less-than-friendly competition between them. Not that he wanted the fame and fortune that came with winning, as he suspected she did; he just wanted respect. A small pug in a big dog world doesn't get a lot of respect; he usually gets run over.

The dog park was abuzz with the news. Carlos and his dog Diablo had arrived in town late last night and, if Snitch was right, a rumble was gonna go down some place real soon. Every dog in Hope Springs had heard of Diablo. He was a mastiff whose previous owner had bled to death when his loving dog attacked him. Every dog was quaking in his paws at the thought of a hoodlum in town, and a Meeting of the Four had been called. Such a thing had never happened as long as Pugsley had been alive, but that wasn't really saying much, since he was only eight in dog years.

There were also other whispers for ears who inclined to gossip, namely that Snitch was now Pet-less. Some malicious butt-stabbers claimed José had skipped town when he found out Carlos was due any day, while others chose to believe the Pet would be found at the bottom of the Hope Springs River. Either way, Snitch was a mess. His coat hadn't been brushed in several days, and his ribs were starting to show. All the dogs were concerned for their friend, and they tried to help as best they could but Snitch would have none of it.

"Been livin' on the streets most of my life. Don't make no diff now, I guess. I'll be fine," was all he said.

The day of the Greatest Tail Ever Dog Show had finally come. Godiva was the first to arrive, as usual, head held high like she owned the place. Herr Pet Isabella was furiously brushing out the Afghan's smooth coat one more time, until it shone in the mid-afternoon sun. As an admitted attention-hog, this was right up her alley. She sighed a contented doggie sigh; as she looked around at the contestants her smile turned to a frown. *He* had arrived.

Pugsley was a small, rather nondescript pug who had little to commend him, but he did have one thing going for him: he was rather proud of his tail. For such a small dog he had inherited the most magnificent tail, and he made sure every dog town knew it. He could curl it and uncurl it on cue, something that delighted the judges and infuriated Godiva.

Unlike some local canines he could mention, he came from a good family with breeding one could trace back 400 years. One of two pugs belonging to the two uncles who lived next door to each other, Pugsley took the word 'snooty' to a whole 'nother level. Pongo was the closest to a friend Pugsley actually had, so it was a good thing he lived right next door.

Godiva snarled as Pugsly sauntered by with his nose

in the air. Victory was in the air; he could feel it in his dog bones. His Pet Zeke was rather large and in definite need of exercise, so Pugsley took the opportunity to make sure he got some.

Caught in the Middle

Word on the tough side of town was that the uncles were coming out of exile. That's what happens when you live in a small town like Hope Springs. Drama makes news. Especially for dogs.

The Pets don't seem to care, but the canines... well, they are all extremely interested.

Finklestein was the first to take the plunge.

"Every dog in town wants to know, dude – what's the deal with the two uncles?"

Pugsley frowned and turned his back on the Border Collie. He had more important things to do today than engage in gossip. This was his big break, and he was going to take it. He walked towards Deke purposefully, brush in his mouth, for one last grooming before his turn in the spotlight.

The pug absent-mindedly thought back to the day he was adopted. He'd heard the rumours, of course, but never took them seriously. His first Pet beat him often, and he was glad when a stranger came to take him away. That stranger turned out to be Deke.

The uncles, Deke and Zeke, had married two Pets, sisters in fact, way, way back before the dawn of time, but both sisters had died in a car accident; the two uncles, who had been riding in the back, survived, and when they came to in the hospital they were devastated. Both uncles determined to never marry again and never leave town, and that's exactly what they did.

Then they decided that was rather a lonely life, so one uncle, Deke, decided to look in the newspaper and found Pugsley, which was how he came to have such a fine home. The other uncle, Zeke, who had gone with his brother out of boredom, decided they couldn't separate friends and promptly bought Pongo on the spot.

Pongo was possibly Pugsley's greatest and definitely most sincere admirer. As such, Pugsley considered it Pongo's duty to support him every year at the Greatest Tail Ever Dog Show; this was how Pongo came to be sitting in his Pet's lap as the Hope Springs High School band started playing, signaling the start of the show. Judges quickly found their places and sat, rather uncomfortably, on the wooden seats behind the roped-off arena designated for dogs.

All the show dogs had skills and abilities, which was why they were there. Pugsley had often thought of learning a routine but Deke never seemed up to the task. The Pet sat around all day staring into space. Sometimes he went next door and did the same at Pongo's house. Pugsley would never understand pets, not even if he lived a thousand years.

The announcer called Godiva's name. She walked proudly around in the grassy arena, showing off her glossy coat and soft ears well. Pugsley glowered. Didn't she have any new tricks?

Actually, she did. Isabella her Pet produced an orange ball from her pocket, and balanced it on Godiva's nose. Delicately, the canine continued to keep it there, on the tip of her nose, to the applause of all onlookers. Pugsley was furious.

She caught the orange ball three times and the crowd went wild.

Godiva left the arena, tail wagging happily, and threw him a haughty look. She didn't even look back to see what points the judges gave her.

Pugsley was ready. He walked as fast as his little legs would carry him all around the grassy area, and sat calmly in front of the judges. Deke gave two short whistles and Pugsley jumped up, turned around, and unfurled his tail. Then he pulled it back. He did this six times, to the delight of the judges. They clapped hard, and told him how wonderful he was. Which he knew, already, but Pets were like that, they always stated the obvious.

He lost to Godiva by one point.

Missing

Nodog had seen José and Snitch was getting worried. His Pet had never up and left without letting Snitch know, and putting the food bowl out, full enough to last till he got back. According to Serious, José had been gone two days now and Snitch was really hungry.

Oakley and Rock lay down in the dog park and had a long woof together. They decided to help Snitch find his Pet, because that's what pals did, stick by each other. So they did. When they saw Snitch outside the gate they whined until their Pets let him in. They bounded up and told him their idea.

Being the tough dog that he was, Snitch would never admit it but he was glad to have help. He had no idea how to find José on his own, and as much as it pained him, he needed pals. Bad.

They made a plan together and all three put one paw in the middle together as a sign of palship. If José could be found, they would find him. If not, they would just help Snitch find another Pet.

Half an hour later Josh brought Leo to the dog park. Snitch couldn't contain himself, he dashed up and licked his bdp on the nose. Josh took a long hard look at Snitch.

"Hey, buddie, come here!" he said, holding out his hand.

Snitch obediently came up and sniffed it.

"I know, bud, José is missing. I'll bet you're hungry. I'll take you home with us tonight till we figure out what to do with you."

He ruffled Snitch's ears, something the little dog was extremely fond of.

Rock and Oakley smiled. With Josh and Leo on the case, José was sure to turn up really soon. They were the best law enforcement team in the business, or so every dog in the dog park thought. Though they'd never tell Leo to his face; he didn't take compliments well.

After a very large meal and a good night's sleep on a dog pillow, Snitch decided he could face one more day. A day that, as it turned out, couldn't have been any worse if it had tried. First of all, Josh didn't fix Snitch his ham and eggs, like José did every morning. It turns out Leo didn't know about ham and eggs. Josh didn't give Leo Pet food. Then the two dogs were left alone all morning cooped up in the house and after a huge dinner and small breakfast Snitch couldn't help it. He had to go.

He sniffed around for the perfect place, and decided it would be best to keep it out in plain view so when Leo's Pet got mad – they always did – he'd be able to clean it up easily.

The two dogs played chase for a while but that got boring. So Leo pulled out his dog toys and shared them with Snitch. But after a while that got boring too.
Hours later Josh finally came home, but he was walking different. Slow. Sad, somehow. He didn't say anything when he found Snitch's accident, just silently cleaned it up. Then he bent down and grabbed the little dog up by the back of his neck, something he hated, and sat down on the couch with Snitch on his lap.

"Buddie," he said, "I've got bad news. Maybe you won't understand but I'll tell you anyway. José is missing. We've searched Hope Springs all day long and no one's seen hide nor hair of him for over three days. I don't know what to do, buddie, I'm all out of ideas. Any suggestions?"

His eyes brimmed with tears as he gently stroked the little white dog. Snitch snuffled softly. He couldn't tell Josh but he understood everything. José was gone. And he might never come back.

🐾

Meet The Characters

Rock – a mutt
His intelligence, endurance and joy in working make him a
great police dog, herder, service dog, therapy dog and
devoted friend; large appetite, very loyal; instinctually
protective, he sits back to watch and wait before he acts;

https://www.pinterest.com/pin/797559415230325772/

Oakley, like this but with quite a bit of grey
Whippet – intelligent, beautiful, easy going, neat and tidy,
fast, stays close to owner's heel, amicable, superb hunter,
cheap to keep, not a fussy eater, loves people, few are equal
to his temperament.

http://www.akc.org/dog-breeds/whippet/

McTavish, white with grey around the jowls
Cairn/Scottish Highland Terrier – engaging, fascinating character, small stature, big heart, bustles everywhere at a great pace; tireless fellow, impressively sharp voice, delights in human company on a country walk or shopping trip; lives a long life, eats what is offered, devil-may-care attitude, bold, willful, loves digging, not greedy, needs exercise, guards his domain noisily, thinks people are there purely for company and for fun.

https://www.pinterest.com/pin/472385448392759587/

Reikah, Mishka and Moutar
Siberian Husky – racer sled dog, looks like a wolf with a kind face, long coat, almost any colour, remarkable eyes, extremely tolerant of people but not his own kind; domineering, distinct pecking order; the odd one can be persuaded to obey at times but it is simply not his idea of how a dog should behave; often exercised by pulling a sled on wheels or rigged up wagon; rarely lowers pricked ears; think carefully before choosing him as a friend; hungry, friendly but reserved.

https://www.pinterest.com/pin/289074869812506237/

Feingold,
Alsatian/German Shepherd –
Strong, courageous, obedient, often used in search-and-rescue units; tenacious, loyal, focused, very protective, courageous, suspicious, curious, watchful, sometimes aggressive; core temperament is inherited, not developed, and never changes fundamentally.

🐾 56

Godiva,
Afghan Hound – elegant,
Great Dane – short dense coat, brindle/fawn/blue/black/ harlequin/white with black/blue patches), strong, wild boar chaser in times past, intelligent but not obedient; independent, aloof, kind, dignified, likes exercise and creature comfort, large appetite, short life span.

http://www.akc.org/dog-breeds/afghan-hound/

Beaker,
Beagle – super friendly, enjoys being part of a gang, solid, sturdy, tidy, not easily housetrained, short waterproof drip-dry coat, not greedy, excellent hunting dogs, long life span, happy-go-lucky, funny, like to follow their nose, stubborn, very active, not always obedient.

http://www.akc.org/dog-breeds/beagle/

Maverick,
Wire Fox Terrier - Alert, quick to move at the slightest opportunity; confident, gregarious, crave attention, deeply loyal; keen expression, ears folded over, lean, muscular, strong; coat mostly white but mixed with brindle/red/liver/slatblue.

http://www.hamsheregallery.co.uk/directory_individual.php?breed=186&search=1&table=breed

Colt,
Boxer – extravert, intelligent, fun-loving, bright, active, believes he knows best, supple limbs and body, muscle, stamina, guards loved ones zealously and will be clear about it; white, believes life should be lived at speed, doesn't starts fights often but never backs down once challenged, biddable and fearless.

https://www.pinterest.com/pin/260371226267468/

Padré
Chihuahua – from South America; long smooth coat, soft and glossy, never coarse; tiny, tremendous spirit, very proud of his tail which he carries high, fawn to red with white is normal colour, brave, endures pain, doesn't take

insults well or humans who invade their home without permission, defiant and threatening mayhem while defending his own; loves exercise, intelligent, undemanding

Chang Po,
Pekinese – roots in Tang Dynasty; occasional glimmer of humour, huge personality, broad head, short muzzle; often has severe breathing problems, not fond of exercise; dignified, leisurely, long profuse coat; needs regular dedicated attention, referred to in Chinese court as "sleeve dogs", almost any colour, affectionate and loyal.

Serious, a rather large ball of fluff
English Sheepdog -

http://www.akc.org/dog-breeds/old-english-sheepdog/
Adaptable, smart, gentle, strong, compact, thickset, muscular, great drover's dog; intelligent expression, ears flat against the head, profuse coat with good texture, agile fluid movement, even-tempered, friendly and courageous.

The General,
Bulldog – aka British Bulldog, stubborn, slow walker, gets hot easily; over-exertion can have serious health consequences but can produce a surprising burst of speed; breathes noisily, bred to grip bulls by the nose with his teeth; short coat, easily cleaned; calm, courageous, friendly; dignified, amusing, massive build; dubbed "Old Sourmug", superb guard dog; adores kids, can ignore or be aggressive to strangers if provoked; affectionate, determined.

Snitch,
Yorkshire Terrier – aptitude for rat-catching, square build, thick coat, needs trimming on a regular basis, very smart dog when well trained; small dark eyes full of fire and intelligence; sprightly, tomboyish, affectionate; big personality, brave, determined, curious and full of energy.

Leo,
Golden Retriever – canine all-rounder, multi-talented, retrieving and blind guide dog/ drugs/explosive detector, laid back, obedient, hard worker, likes to eat so watch his waistline, easy to train, needs stimulation, easily bored,

good at steady thoughtful walking, generous, loving, intelligent, biddable.

Gunny,
(Miniature) Schnauzer – harsh wiry coat, groomed with a wire glove, loves children, black/black and silver/ salt and pepper, luxurious eyebrows and beard, does everything "on the double", quiet, great for busy families or older adults; alert, intelligent; will never refuse exercise no matter how much is offered, hair grows to extraordinary lengths, regular trimming essential; useful warning signal due to loudish bark.

http://www.akc.org/dog-breeds/standard-schnauzer/

Finklestein,
Border Collie – smart, likes to work, athletic, neat, agile; overactive brain can lead to mischief if not kept busy, thinks on his feet; runs fast in a permanent crouch, demands exercise for both body and brain; will nip to make a point, very alert and trainable, tireless.

www.akc.org

Sugar,
Pit Bull – actually called the Staffordshire Bull Terrier; strong, muscular, agile; short coarse coat, graceful; alert, aware, friendly, indomitably courageous, highly intelligent,

outgoing, tenacious; strong-willed, affectionate, loyal.

Pugsley
Pug - described as "multum in parvo" (a lot of dog in a
small space); even-tempered, playful, outgoing, loving;
charming, mischievous, endlessly curious, barks when
necessary.

https://www.pinterest.com/pin/344525440215891641/

CrossEffective Publishing©   copyright 2000